D1093257

CHURCHMOUSE STORIES

MARGOT AUSTIN'S
CHURCHMOUSE STORIES

A Collection of
Peter Churchmouse
And Other Children's Favorites

Illustrated by the Author

E. P. DUTTON & CO., INC.
NEW YORK

Library of Congress Catalog Card Number: 56-8291

PETER CHURCHMOUSE

S - N - A - P! went the snap-rat.

PETER CHURCHMOUSE

Up jumped Peter!

S-N-A-P! went the snap-rat!

Poor little Peter Churchmouse raised his eyebrows the way he always did when he made a poem,

> "I wish the cheese I ate
> Were on a plate
> That wouldn't snap at me
> Because I DON'T LIKE IT!"

Then Peter sat right down on the big wooden snap-rat and ate his cheese. Every last bit.

"Now," said Peter, "I shall bite another big hole in something so that Parson Pease-Porridge will put more cheese on the snap-rat for tomorrow."

So Peter ate a great big hole in the red felt that lined arson Pease-Porridge's best collection basket.

"There," said Peter, "Parson Pease-Porridge will be ire to notice that!"

"I'll be twitched," said Parson Pease-Porridge next morning when he saw the great big hole that Peter had made in the best collection basket.

"These holes will be the ruination of me. I must do something drastic! I'll show these rats—I'll get a *cat!!*"

"Oh-h-h," said Peter Churchmouse. "Oh-h-h, poor me!"

Then Peter Churchmouse raised his eyebrows the way he always did when he thought of a poem,

> "I believe I heard
> That terrible word
> I'm scared to tell it
> So I'll only spell it—
> C-A-T!"

Next day Peter looked for cheese on the snap-rat as usual.

But the snap-rat was gone and in its place was a bowl of milk. And beside the bowl of milk was Gabriel.

"Hello," said Peter stepping bravely from behind the organ, "I'm afraid of cats. Are you a cat?"

"Who? Me?" said Gabriel sitting up. "I'm not a cat. I'm a kitten and my name's Gabriel. Are you a rat?"

"Of course not," said Peter. "I'm a poor Church-mouse and my name is Peter."

"Hello, Peter," said Gabriel. "I'm to scare the rats away. The rats who've been eating big holes in things. Do you know how to scare rats?"

"No I don't," said Peter. "And if I did it wouldn't help you because there aren't any rats here at all. There's only poor me. I pretend I'm rats. *I* bite the great big holes in everything!"

"You don't!" said Gabriel.

"I do," said Peter. "Once I even ate a hymn book. It tasted awful."

"For pity's sake," said Gabriel in a shocked voice. "Cover and all?"

"Cover and all," said Peter. "And I didn't like to do it."

"Then why *did* you do it?" asked Gabriel.

"Because I was hungry," said Peter. "I'm *always* hungry!"

"How sad for you," said Gabriel. "Parson Pease-Porridge gives *me* lots to eat."

"That's because you're a big kitten and he can see you," cried poor Peter. "But I'm a little mouse and he can't see me at all. He's too near-sighted! He doesn't even know I live here. And now that you've come even the snap-rat is gone. All I ever got to eat was the cheese on the snap-rat, and I wouldn't have got that if Parson Pease-Porridge didn't think I was the rats that make the holes *I* bite in things. Fuss, fuss, fuss. Oh, I don't like it!"

"How very sad," said Gabriel. "How very, very sad."

"Sad indeed," said Peter. "I even make poems about it."

13

"I'd like to hear one, please," said Gabriel.

"Gladly," said Peter, raising his eyebrows. "One goes like this—

Snap, whack, bang,
Goes the snap-rat bang,
Goes snap bang,
Goes whack bang,
Fuss, fuss, fuss!"

"It's a beautiful poem," said Gabriel admiringly. "I could listen and listen and listen."

"Thank you kindly," said Peter.

"Maybe I can help you think of a way to let Parson Pease-Porridge know he has a poor hungry Churchmouse," said Gabriel. "So you'll get lots to eat like I do."

"But how?" said Peter.

"I really don't know," said Gabriel. "I'll think very hard."

"Please do," said Peter. "Think hard while I have a lick of your milk."

15

So Peter played hide-behind-the-hymn-book on the shelf where the hymn books were kept. And Gabriel played chew-the-toe with Parson Pease-Porridge's old black slipper. And they both played slide-up-and-down the pew bench.

And all the while Peter longed and longed for cheese. And all the while Gabriel thought and thought about how he could help poor Peter. But Gabriel couldn't think of a single way.

"Listen, Gabriel," said Peter at last.

"I am," said Gabriel. "I'm listening."

"That's fine," said Peter, "Because *I* have an idea about how I can get Parson Pease-Porridge to notice me."

"And get some cheese," added Gabriel.

"Well," said Peter. "I've heard Parson Pease-Porridge say that little children who drink lots of milk grow up to be big children, and you're a big kitten so it must be because you drink lots of milk. So *maybe* if I drink lots of milk I'll grow so big that Parson Pease-Porridge will be able to see me!"

"I *am* a big kitten," admitted Gabriel. "So that must be the reason. Help yourself to some more of my milk."

"Thank you," said Peter between licks, "I much prefer cheese but I'll take anything, even milk, if only Parson Pease-Porridge will notice me!"

"I'll be twitched," remarked Parson Pease-Porridge. "I never knew a kitten to drink so much milk!"

For Peter drank and drank and drank Gabriel's milk every day. And every day he asked Gabriel if he had grown any bigger. And every day he looked in the mirror over the organ to see if he looked any bigger. And every day Gabriel measured him alongside Parson Pease-Porridge's ink bottle to see if he stretched any bigger—but he didn't. Not one bit.

"Except," said Gabriel, "your waist is nearly as round as the ink bottle."

"It's no use," said poor Peter, "no use at all."

"Make a poem about it," said Gabriel.

"Very well," said Peter, lifting his eyebrows—

"Drink, drink, drink,
    To make me bigger,
    But all I do
    Is lose my figure.
    Fuss, fuss, fuss!"

"How beautiful," said Gabriel. "I could listen and listen."

Peter stopped dancing on the black notes of the organ and looked over the edge of the keyboard at Gabriel.

"Gabriel, do you know what?" asked Peter.

Gabriel stopped sharpening his nails on the organ's green carpet pedals and looked up at Peter.

"I don't," said Gabriel.

"I have another idea, that's what!" said Peter. "About how I can get Parson Pease-Porridge to notice me."

"And get some cheese," added Gabriel.

"If," said Peter, waving his arms, "Parson Pease-Porridge saw my nice red knitted bed he'd know it was much too small for rats to sleep in. So he'd know right off that a little Churchmouse slept in it. Wouldn't he?"

"Quite true," agreed Gabriel. "And it's such a beautiful bed, too."

"It *is* a nice bed," said Peter. "We'll put it beside his black leather book so he'll be sure to see it."

"We'll do it right now," said Gabriel, "because I've heard Parson Pease-Porridge say 'never put off till tomorrow what you can do right now.'"

So Peter and Gabriel laid the red knitted bed right beside the big black leather book.

"There," said Peter, "Parson Pease-Porridge will be *sure* to notice that!"

"I'll be twitched," said Parson Pease-Porridge when he saw Peter's knitted bed beside his black leather book.

"How in the world did my old red mitten get here? I've been hunting for that good red mitten for ages. Hem-mmp! I'm a forgetful old man! So I'll just put this mitten in my pocket so I won't lose it again. Hemp, hemp-p-p!"

And away went Parson Pease-Porridge with Peter's bed.

22

"How very, very sad," said Gabriel. "Now your bed's gone."

"It's the only bed I had," said poor little Peter. "The only bed I *ever* had."

"You *should* make a poem about it," encouraged Gabriel.

"I will," said Peter lifting his eyebrows—

> "I had a bed,
> My bed was red.
> Now it's gone,
> I have no place to rest my head.
> It's gone—my lovely bed!"

"It's a beautiful poem," said Gabriel. "It's so sad, I could listen and listen and listen."

"Peter, do you know what?" asked Gabriel.

"I do not," said Peter who was sniffing the flowers that stood on Parson Pease-Porridge's desk.

START

"I have an idea," answered Gabriel, "that will be *sure* to get Parson Pease-Porridge to notice you."

"So I'll get some cheese," said Peter. "Hurry and tell me."

"It's this," said Gabriel. "If you stood right under Parson Pease-Porridge's nose he'd have to see you. Wouldn't he?"

"True," said Peter. "But how *can* I stand right under Parson Pease-Porridge's nose? He's much too tall."

"It's really quite simple," said Gabriel. "When Parson Pease-Porridge sits at his desk to read his big black book it's right under his nose. So if you jump out of those flowers, plop, onto the big black book you'll be right under his nose, too. Then if you'll stand very still he'll be sure to notice you."

"True, true," said Peter. "I'll climb into the flowers right now."

"Do hurry," whispered Gabriel. "Parson Pease-Porridge is coming!"

"Hum-mp," said Parson Pease-Porridge sitting down at his desk.

"Hemp, hem-mmp," said Parson Pease-Porridge opening his big black leather book.

"Now," whispered Peter to himself. "Now is the time!"

So plop, jumped Peter, plump in the middle. Right under Parson Pease-Porridge's nose!

"And *now*," said Peter to himself, "Parson Pease-Porridge will be *sure* to notice me."

"I'll be twitched," said Parson Pease-Porridge, pushing up his spectacles. "What's this? Oh, I'm a bothered old man.

"I'll be twitched," said Parson Pease-Porridge, pushing his spectacles down again. "I see a grey spot before my eyes!

"I must have my glasses changed," said he, closing his big book with a terrible—

B—A—N—G!

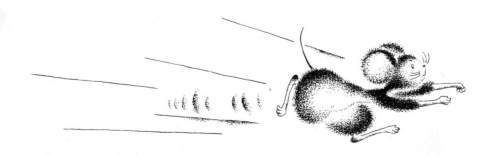

"Oh-h-h," gasped Peter. "Oh-h, poor me."

"He thought you were a grey spot," said Gabriel.

"I might have been," said Peter.

"Very true," said Gabriel. "How awful!"

"I shall make a poem about it," said Peter raising his eyebrows—

> "I jumped quick
> When the book closed whang.
> I learned the trick
> On the snap-rat bang.
> Fuss, fuss, fuss!"

"Very lovely," sighed Gabriel. "I could listen and listen."

"I have another idea," said Gabriel.

"About how I can get Parson Pease-Porridge to notice me so I'll get cheese?" asked Peter.

"That's right," said Gabriel.

"Then please stop playing jump-over-the-pew-bench," said Peter, "because I'm listening."

"It's this," said Gabriel. "I'll spill Parson Pease-Porridge's ink bottle. Then you can walk in the ink and make foot-prints on his big white blotter, and when he sees your little foot-prints he'll know you're a little Churchmouse."

"Then I'll get cheese," said Peter. "Cheese!"

"Quite true," said Gabriel. "Follow me."

So up they jumped onto Parson Pease-Porridge's desk. Gabriel gave the ink bottle a big push. Over it went and out came the ink.

"Now," said Gabriel. "Make some tracks."

"I will," said Peter running right through the ink and right onto Parson Pease-Porridge's clean white blotter. And he went round and round and round.

"Stop, Peter!" cried Gabriel. "Stop!"

"Why?" asked Peter.

"Because," cried Gabriel, "look what's happening!"

For every step poor Peter took on the blotter was spreading bigger and bigger.

"Don't make more prints. Parson Pease-Porridge will think I've done it," cried Gabriel. "Quick! Dry your feet on something!"

"I'll dry my feet here," said Peter, jumping from the blotter to the sermon that Parson Pease-Porridge had finished writing that very morning.

"Hurry, hurry," cried Gabriel. "Here comes Parson Pease-Porridge. We'd better go!"

"Fuss, fuss, fuss," said Peter wiping his feet very hard all along the bottom of Parson Pease-Porridge's sermon.

"I'll be twitched," said Parson Pease-Porridge, "Gabriel has spilled my ink! Tut, tut, look at his big tracks on my blotter!

"Tut, tut, *tut,*" said Parson Pease-Porridge looking from the blotter to his sermon, "I'm a bothered old man. It seems I've made foot-notes on the bottom of my sermon, but I can't seem to read them. Hem-mp! That settles it. I *must* have my glasses changed this *very* day.

"A pretty pass!" said Parson Pease-Porridge as he hurried away. "Can't even read my *own* foot-notes!"

"It's no use," said Peter. "Parson Pease-Porridge will never notice me. Never."

"And you'll never get any cheese," added Gabriel.

"But I *must* have cheese," cried Peter.

"How sad for you," said Gabriel. "Make a poem about it."

"I shall," said Peter lifting his eyebrows—

> "Oh, please, please,
> I want cheese.
> I'm sad, sad,
> I wish I had
> Cheese, Cheese, CHEESE!"

"Lovely," said Gabriel. "I could listen and listen."

"Gabriel," said Peter, "I'm going to bite a hole in something!"

"Oh, do!" encouraged Gabriel. "Do bite something!"

"I will," said Peter. "I'll bite a hole right through the middle of Parson Pease-Porridge's sermon! Then he'll notice me!"

So Peter began to bite and bite right through the middle of Parson Pease-Porridge's sermon.

"Oh my, it's the biggest hole I've ever seen," admired Gabriel, when Peter had finished.

"It's the biggest hole I ever bit," said Peter.

The next day Parson Pease-Porridge had a new pair of spectacles that were three times as thick and three times as strong as his old ones.

"Hem-mp," said he. "It's fine to have new spectacles. I can see everything. I believe I'll have a look at my sermon!

"I'll be twitched," cried Parson Pease-Porridge when he saw the *tremendous* hole in the middle of his sermon. "Oh ruination! Oh, I'm a bothered old man!"

And *then* Parson Pease-Porridge looked at the foot-notes that he couldn't read the day before.

"Upon my soul," cried Parson Pease-Porridge. "These are *not* foot-notes, these are foot-prints! Little foot-prints! I have a Churchmouse! Poor little thing he's eaten all these holes to show me he's hungry!"

"Hem-m-mp," said Parson Pease-Porridge. "Owing to this slight accident (here Parson Pease-Porridge looked at the hole in his sermon) I must abandon the text I prepared for today. So I shall speak about KIND-NESS instead. KINDNESS to very little animals.

"And now," smiled Parson Pease-Porridge, "never put off till tomorrow what you can do right now!

"I must get CHEESE for my Churchmouse!"

"Oh-h, Gabriel," whispered Peter. "Did you hear that?"

"I did," said Gabriel. "Parson Pease-Porridge has noticed you at last!"

"Oh, poor me," cried Peter. "I'm going to get cheese after all!"

"Quite true," replied Gabriel.

"I'll make a little poem about it," said Peter lifting his eyebrows the way he always did—

> "Cheese,
> Cheese, cheese,
> Cheese, cheese, cheese,
> C—H—E—E—S—E !"

"How beautiful," sighed Gabriel. "I could listen and listen and listen."

THE END

GABRIEL CHURCHKITTEN

GABRIEL CHURCHKITTEN

"Don't breathe!"

"Don't move!"

"Don't do anything!" commanded Gabriel Church-kitten.

"Why not?" asked his friend, Peter Churchmouse.

"Because," whispered Gabriel, "*I'm* thinking."

"Silliest thing I ever heard," fussed Peter—

> "You're all fluff
> And no stuff.
> You haven't enough
> To think with!"

"I have too," said Gabriel. "Look at *me*!"

"Well, for pity's sake," cried Peter staring at Gabriel. "What's that thing tied on your head?"

"*That*," said Gabriel, "is my thinking-hat!"

"Your *thinking-hat*!" cried Peter. "What kind of hat is that?"

"The kind you put on to do your thinking," explained Gabriel, "when you haven't much to think with."

"Like the thinking-cap that Parson Pease-Porridge says he puts on when he writes a sermon?" asked Peter.

"Exactly," beamed Gabriel.

"Indeed," said Peter. "Where did you get it?"

"In Parson Pease-Porridge's cupboard," confided Gabriel, "hanging on a tree in a round glass box. It fits me fine, doesn't it?"

"Indeed," repeated Peter. "What's that stuffed bird sitting on it for?"

"Well," said Gabriel, "only yesterday Parson Pease-Porridge said a little bird told him who took the pink bath soap."

"True," agreed Peter, absently chewing a candle. "It was *very* bracing soap."

"So," boasted Gabriel, "*my* little bird is going to tell *me* things, too. Important things! Like how to stop Parson Pease-Porridge from having a snack—"

"And keeping us awake all night playing on the organ?" cried Peter, dropping the candle and gluing his eyes to Gabriel's hat.

"Exactly," said Gabriel. "Think, think, *think!* I think it's awful cold tonight, even with my fur coat on."

"So what?" said Peter. "We're not going out."

"I know," said Gabriel. "But if we would open the side door when Parson Pease-Porridge gets up tonight, the cold wind could blow right in on his bare ankles. Then Parson Pease-Porridge would be so cold he'd go right back to bed again, wouldn't he?"

"I expect he would," said Peter. "But we *can't* open the side door because we *can't* reach the latch."

"Yes, we can. With the candle-lighter-snuffer," said Gabriel, marching straight to Parson Pease-Porridge's cupboard and thumping about till he found it.

"Hurry," encouraged Peter, "I hear Parson Pease-Porridge getting into bed."

"I am hurrying," puffed Gabriel, hooking the lighter-snuffer over the latch and jerking open the door.

Whew-w-w-w-w came a gust of ice cold wind!

"Just in time," gasped Gabriel, for Parson Pease-Porridge had snored only once when, squeek squeep, went the bed springs.

Parson Pease-Porridge was getting right up again!

"Draughty-dr-r-aughty," murmured he between little snores.

"Draugh-h-h-ty," murmured he, getting slowly out of bed and scuffing into his slippers.

"F-feed-churchmouse-feed-kitten," snored he, moving slowly away with his arms stretched out before him.

"C-cheese-for-churchmouse," murmured he, putting cheese on Peter's little plate.

"M-milk-for-kitten," murmured he, filling Gabriel's bowl.

"N-now-snack-snack," murmured he, between snores.

And then Parson Pease-Porridge took the cheese from Peter's plate and ate every bit of it.

And *then* Parson Pease-Porridge sipped every drop of Gabriel's milk.

"N-*now*-music—m-u-s-i-c," murmured he, sitting down at the organ and beginning to play with one finger.

"He doesn't seem to mind cold ankles a bit," shivered Gabriel. "He's playing *every* psalm he knows!"

"Exactly," agreed Peter. "And it sounds dreadful."

"You're quite right," came a voice from the open doorway.

"What's that?" cried Peter, leaping behind Gabriel.

"*That*," said Gabriel, looking very fierce, "is a big *dog* with three spots. And I'm not supposed to like spotted dogs."

"Why not?" asked Peter.

"Because," frowned Gabriel.

"Then *I* shall speak to him," said Peter, stepping out from behind Gabriel. "What's your name, dog?"

"My name's Trumpet, and what's on your friend's head?"

"My thinking-hat," beamed Gabriel, forgetting he wasn't supposed to like Trumpet. "To think things with."

"What kinds of things?" asked Trumpet as he helped Gabriel and Peter push the side door shut.

"Important things," said Peter waving his arms, "like—

> Why—
> Does poor Parson P.
> Snore 1, 2, 3
> Instead of 1234567
> Clear to eleven?"

"I wouldn't know why," answered Trumpet. "But, I'd like to meet Parson P."

"You will," said Peter, curling up in an old red mitten. "Just make yourself at home."

"While we *try* to nap," yawned Gabriel.

"I shall," said Trumpet, curling up beside Gabriel. "And thank you."

"A *bone*," breathed Trumpet.

"How's that?" asked Peter, waking up from his nap.

"A bone," smiled Trumpet. "Parson Pease-Porridge is going to give *me* a big bone when he feeds you and Gabriel."

"Don't be too sure," warned Gabriel, waking up with a start.

"Why not?" asked Trumpet. "Parson Pease-Porridge *said* so."

"You'll see tonight," said Gabriel, tilting his hat over his eyes. "And I've been thinking again—"

"About how to stop Parson Pease-Porridge from keeping us awake and having a snack?" asked Peter.

"Exactly," answered Gabriel. "It's like this: when Parson Pease-Porridge gets out of bed he always puts on his slippers, doesn't he?"

"True," agreed Peter.

"So," said Gabriel, briskly tapping his hat, "if Parson Pease-Porridge didn't have his slippers he couldn't walk, could he?"

"No," said Peter. "He couldn't."

"How strange," said Trumpet.

"And if he couldn't walk, he'd have to stay in bed, wouldn't he?" mused Gabriel. "So, we'll hide his slippers as soon as he snores even once."

"And we'll hide us quick," cried Peter. "Because I hear Parson Pease-Porridge coming!"

"Ho-hum-rummer," yawned Parson Pease-Porridge as he turned back the covers. "Dear-o-dearie, but it's nice to go to bed when one's as tired as I am."

"Hum-um-umer but I'm bothered," said he, kicking off his slippers. "I get up tired every morning, and I haven't any appetite, and all night long I seem to hear music!"

"Rum-um-ummer," said he, pulling up the covers. "Now I lay me down to s-l-e-e-p——"

"And *now*," said Peter, lifting his eyebrows the way he always did when he made up a poem——

"Snore, snore
Snore some more——"

"Stop it," whispered Gabriel, "and help us hide these slippers before Parson Pease-Porridge gets up again."

"Oh, very well," said Peter, tugging away with the others.

"Just in time!" gasped Gabriel, for Parson Pease-Porridge had snored only twice when, squeek squeep, went the bed springs.

"He's getting up again," whispered Peter.

"To get me a *bone*," chimed in Trumpet.

"C-co-o-old-slipper's-cold," murmured Parson Pease-Porridge between little snores.

"C-c-o-o-l-d," murmured he, putting a foot in the place where one slipper *should* have been.

"Ccc-o-o-ld," murmured he, and with another little snore, he put the other foot where the *other* slipper should have been.

"F-feed-mouse-feed-kitten-feed-dog," snored he.

And away he walked in his *bare* feet, with his arms stretched out before him.

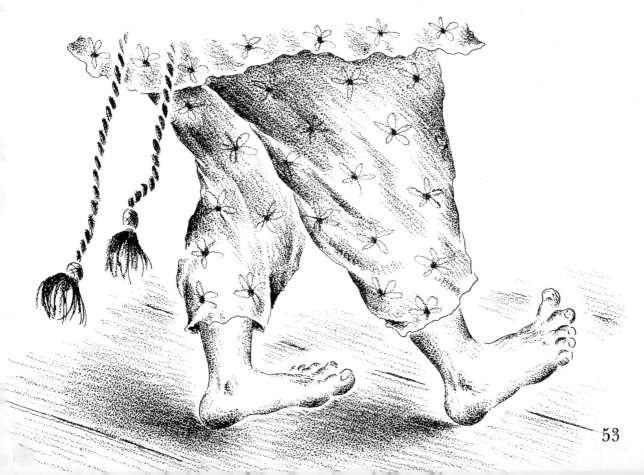

"M-m-must-feed-mouse," snored Parson Pease-Por-ridge, putting cheese on Peter's little plate.

"How kind," said Trumpet.

"F-feed-kitten," murmured Parson Pease-Porridge, filling Gabriel's bowl to the very brim.

"How *very* kind," exclaimed Trumpet.

"Now-feed-d-d-o-g," murmured Parson Pease-Porridge. "Feed-dog-bone."

And he put a large juicy bone on a plate for Trumpet.

"How wonderful!" gasped Trumpet. "It's for me! My bone!"

"True, true," sighed Gabriel and Peter together.

"And-n-now-snack-snack-snack," snored Parson Pease-Porridge, munching every last crumb of Peter's cheese.

"How sad," grieved Trumpet.

Then "Mm-m-mum," murmured Parson Pease-Por-ridge, sipping every last drop of Gabriel's milk.

"Poor Gabriel," gasped Trumpet.

Then "Mm bone-bone," murmured Parson Pease-Porridge, and he took up Trumpet's bone and began to nibble away!

"Oh-h," cried Trumpet with tears in his eyes. "Oh, poor, poor me!"

"Quite true," agreed Gabriel and Peter as Parson Pease-Porridge sat down at the organ and began to play with one finger.

"It didn't work," said Peter as they tugged Parson Pease-Porridge's slippers back to where they should have been.

"No," said Gabriel, "It didn't work——

I sat, sat, sat,
Under my thinking-hat
But it didn't work at all."

"Gabriel!" cried Peter, "*I'm* supposed to make up poems—not *you*!"

"I'm sorry," said Gabriel, "very sorry."

"Fuss, fuss," fretted Peter, staring at his little empty plate. "Besides having a snack, Parson Pease-Porridge kept us awake again—all night long. He did it the night before too, and the night before that, and the night before that, and the—"

"Be calm," smiled Gabriel, "I feel funny up here."

"Are you thinking?" asked Trumpet.

"Yes," said Gabriel, pushing his hat from his right ear to his left ear. "It's this: Parson Pease-Porridge can't walk a step without bumping into things when he doesn't have his glasses."

"Not a *step*," agreed Peter.

"How strange," said Trumpet.

"Exactly," said Gabriel. "And he always puts his glasses on the table when he goes to bed."

"Yes, yes," fussed Peter. "Go on."

"So," explained Gabriel, "if we put his glasses where he couldn't find them, he'd have to go right back to bed again, wouldn't he?"

"He would," gasped Peter. "And he's coming to bed right now!"

"Ho-hummer," yawned Parson Pease-Porridge, putting his glasses on the little table beside the bed.

"Dearie, but I'm weary," yawned he, pulling the covers up to his chin. "And now I lay me down to s-l-e-e-p——"

Then out stole Gabriel and Peter and Trumpet!

Whisk! They snatched up the glasses and away they went.

For "Feed-mouse-feed-kitten-feed-dog," murmured Parson Pease-Porridge, slowly getting out of bed again and slowly moving off with his arms raised before him.

Then "S-snack-snack-snack," murmured he, having everything he'd put out for Peter and Gabriel and Trumpet.

And then, "M-m-u-s-i-c," mumbled Parson Pease-

Porridge, sitting down at his organ to play every single psalm he knew.

"He didn't need them at *all,*" said Gabriel, putting Parson Pease-Porridge's glasses back on the table.

"Of course not," cried Peter. "Because he kept his eyes closed tight!"

"True," sighed Trumpet, "quite true."

"Don't-breathe-move-or-anything," shouted Gabriel.

"I can't" worried Peter, "because you're sitting on my tail. Are you thinking?"

"I *am*," said Gabriel. "We *can't* stop Parson Pease-Porridge from having a snack but we *can* stop him from playing the organ!"

"How?" asked Trumpet.

"It's *too* simple," said Gabriel. "When Parson Pease-Porridge tries to play the organ tonight it won't make a sound!"

"Why won't it?" asked Peter, staring at Gabriel.

"Because," said Gabriel, "we'll fill all the music holes inside the organ so not a bit of music can leak out."

"What with?" asked Peter.

"Gum," beamed Gabriel.

"That good gum that's sticking under all the pew benches?" asked Trumpet.

"Exactly," breathed Gabriel.

"Then get off my tail so we can start right now," fussed Peter. "There's a big lot of holes."

"True, true," agreed Gabriel as they began to pull gum from the nearest pew bench.

That night Gabriel and Peter and Trumpet watched Parson Pease-Porridge go to bed as usual.

"Now he's getting up again," said Gabriel as Parson Pease-Porridge slowly rose from his bed.

"Now he's putting cheese on my little plate," whispered Peter.

"And milk in Gabriel's bowl and a juicy bone on *my* plate," gulped Trumpet.

"*Now* he's having a snack," sighed Peter and Gabriel and Trumpet.

"As usual," whispered Gabriel. "But he *won't* play the organ as usual."

"No," smiled Peter and Trumpet. "He won't."

"M-m-music," murmured Parson Pease-Porridge,

pressing the organ keys with one finger. But not a sound did the organ make.

"M-m-m," murmured he, pressing the keys still harder.

"We can *sleep*," whispered Gabriel.

But Gabriel was wrong.

For "M-must-have- m-u-s-i-c," murmured Parson Pease Porridge between little snores. "Sing-m-m-music — sing-psalms."

And Parson Pease-Porridge began to sing!

On and on, all through the night.

"You were somewhat wrong last night," remarked Peter as he helped Gabriel and Trumpet pry a bit of gum out of a music hole.

"True," said Gabriel, pasting another bit of gum back under a pew bench. "Parson Pease-Porridge never even missed the organ music."

"And besides, it was much better than the kind he sings," cried Peter.

"*Much* better," said Trumpet.

"Very true," admitted Gabriel. "We'd better hurry or Parson Pease-Porridge will sing again to-night."

"Exactly," said Peter, hastily removing another bit of gum from a music hole and hurriedly putting it back under a pew-bench.

"Look at *me*!" shouted Gabriel.

"Oh-h-h, ooow!" gasped Peter. "For a moment I almost imagined you were a C-A-T instead of a big kitten! Whatever made you make such a nasty face?"

"Well," boasted Gabriel, "I often make frightfully dreadful faces when I'm thinking hard. I practice in the mirror over the organ."

"Indeed," said Peter. "What for?"

"*Because*," whispered Gabriel, beginning once more to make his terrible face——

"Don't do it again!" cried Peter and Trumpet, backing away.

"Very well, I won't," said Gabriel, pulling his hat clear over his ears. "I've been thinking hard all day till my head hurts——"

"But you haven't thought of anything?" worried Peter.

"Not a thing," sighed Gabriel.

"Then *I* won't stand it any longer," cried Trumpet, "To-night *I'm* going to do something *desperate*!"

"You *can't* do that," cried Peter.

"It wouldn't be *polite*," whispered Gabriel.

"I don't care!" shouted Trumpet.

"*Please* stop shouting," fussed Peter. "I hear Parson Pease-Porridge coming!"

"Oh, think!" cried Gabriel, thumping his hat till the dust flew. "Think, think! Parson Pease-Porridge is getting into bed!"

"Think some more," encouraged Peter, "because he's getting up again!"

"F-feed-mouse-kitten-dog," murmured Parson Pease-Porridge, slowly getting out of bed and gliding away with his arms stretched out before him.

"C-ch-e-e-e-se," murmured he, placing cheese on Peter's plate.

"M-m-milk," murmured he, filling Gabriel's bowl.

"B-b-bone-bone," murmured he, putting a juicy bone on Trumpet's plate.

"N-n-now," murmured he, "Snack-sn-a-a-ck-sn———"

"No, no," quavered Trumpet.

"Be calm," whispered Peter, catching hold of Trumpet's fur coat.

"I can't," sobbed Trumpet. "I'm going to *snatch* my bone and run—"

"Think quick, Gabriel!" gasped Peter. "*Think!*"

"I have it," cried Gabriel, taking a tremendous breath and blowing hard——

"Ph-h-h-h-pheew-wufff-ft!"

Right in Trumpet's ear!

"O-oww-wower-wowww!" howled Trumpet, louder than anything.

"Ow-ww-h-ww-wwl!" howled Trumpet even louder. "Ow-w-w! Stop it, oww-wow-wow!!"

"*Oh, ruination!*" cried poor Parson Pease-Porridge, staggering back against the organ.

"Oh, lack-a-day," cried he, blinking about him.

"*I'll be twitched!*" cried he, and his eyes flew wide open!

"No wonder I'm so tired and haven't any appetite!

"*I've been walking in my sleep!!*"

"Just think," said Gabriel. "Our Parson Pease-Porridge was walking in his sleep."

"All the time," said Peter, clutching his cheese.

"Till *I* woke him up with my how-w-wling," boasted Trumpet licking his bone.

"When *I* blew in your ear," smiled Gabriel, over his milk bowl.

"Exactly," agreed Peter. "How did you *ever* think of it?"

"It was *too* simple," said Gabriel, carefully putting his thinking-hat back in the round glass box.

"Yes-yes, go on," admired Peter and Trumpet.

"Well," said Gabriel, blushing modestly, "I sim remembered that once I heard Parson Pease-Porr say '*In the end, Gabriel shall blow on Trumpet*!' "

"Yes-yes," encouraged Peter and Trumpet.

"So," beamed Gabriel, "I just blew!"

THE END

72

"Just think," said Gabriel. "Our Parson Pease-Porridge was walking in his sleep."

"All the time," said Peter, clutching his cheese.

"Till *I* woke him up with my how-w-wling," boasted Trumpet licking his bone.

"When *I* blew in your ear," smiled Gabriel, over his milk bowl.

"Exactly," agreed Peter. "How did you *ever* think of it?"

"It was *too* simple," said Gabriel, carefully putting his thinking-hat back in the round glass box.

"Yes-yes, go on," admired Peter and Trumpet.

"Well," said Gabriel, blushing modestly, "I sim remembered that once I heard Parson Pease-Porr say '*In the end, Gabriel shall blow on Trumpet!*'"

"Yes-yes," encouraged Peter and Trumpet.

"So," beamed Gabriel, "I just blew!"

THE END

TRUMPET

TRUMPET

"Yow-wow-owl," howled Trumpet Churchdog.

"*Don't* do that," cried Gabriel Churchkitten.

"We don't like it!" shouted little Peter Churchmouse.

"I don't either," sighed Trumpet, "but, I just can't help it! Ow-owl!"

"For pity's sakes!" cried Peter, lifting his eyebrows the way he always did when he made a poem —

> "Stop it,
> STOP IT
> *S T O P   I T*
> Or I'll call a coppit!"

"Lovely!" admired Gabriel. "What's a coppit?"

"I wouldn't know," fussed Peter. "Only Trumpet *must* stop that *awful* howling!"

75

"*We* don't like it," went on Peter. "Parson Pease-Porridge won't like it, either!"

"True, true," agreed Gabriel. "And Parson Pease-Porridge is very *kind* to us. He even writes sermons about kindness. Kindness to little animals like us!"

"Very well, then," cried Peter, waving his arms. "We're happy here with Parson Pease-Porridge and we have *cheese!* Think of that!"

"I am," sighed Gabriel. "I'm thinking of milk!"

"I'm thinking, too," sighed Trumpet. "I'm thinking of bones. Oh, ow-owl!"

"There!" shouted Peter, pointing his finger at Trumpet, "there you go again! Why, Parson Pease-Porridge might even send us *all* away — if *you* don't stop howling!!"

"How *sad*," cried Gabriel.

"How *very* sad for us," cried Trumpet. "Oh, wowl!"

"Maybe Trumpet's howling because he has a cold," said Gabriel.

"That's it!" cried Peter. "And Parson Pease-Porridge always says the *only* thing that helps a cold is a big mustard plaster."

"How strange," said Trumpet. "What's a mustard plaster?"

"It's quite simple," said Peter. "We just plaster mustard all over your chest."

"Is that right?" gulped Trumpet.

"Then what are we waiting for?" asked Gabriel. "I'll get the mustard from Parson Pease-Porridge's cupboard."

"But my chest feels fine," cried Trumpet.

"Stand still," fussed Peter, waving the wooden spoon that Gabriel brought with the mustard.

"While we take turns," cried Gabriel, smearing away on Trumpet's chest. "And please don't wiggle."

"I don't like it," cried Trumpet.

"Even so," insisted Peter, "it's for your own good."

"I *still* don't like it," wailed Trumpet. "Oh, wowl!"

"Do stop!" cried Peter. "Here comes Parson Pease-Porridge!"

"Maybe he's going to send us away," whispered Gabriel. "Come on, Peter, let's hide!"

"Well, I'll be twitched," cried Parson Pease-Porridge when he saw Trumpet. "What have we here? What's all this trouble? Why it seems to be mustard!"

"Tut-tut," cried Parson Pease-Porridge, adjusting his spectacles, "you're plastered with mustard! *You'll* be the ruination of me! *Now* I shall have to give you a bath!"

"Dearie, but I'm a bothered old body," sighed Parson Pease-Porridge, scrubbing away on poor Trumpet with a big brush and pink soap.

"How sad," sighed Gabriel. "All that lovely mustard is quite wasted!"

"True," agreed Peter. "And now Parson Pease-Porridge is wasting that *tasty* pink soap!"

"Did you hear that?" asked Peter, leaping out of Parson Pease-Porridge's old black slipper.

"I did," said Gabriel, sliding down a hymn book.

"It's Trumpet," said Peter. "He's howling *again*!"

"Awful loud," said Gabriel, sliding once more down the hymn book.

"Quite true," agreed Peter. "Maybe a stomach-ache."

"Oh, poor Trumpet," gasped Gabriel. "Parson Pease-Porridge *always* takes a hot-water bottle for a stomach-ache."

"The very thing," cried Peter. "Only we'll use a milk bottle instead."

"*My* milk bottle," beamed Gabriel. "But what'll make it hot?"

"Put *pepper* in it," said Peter —

> "A dash of pepper
> From the pot,
> Will make the bottle
> *Hot, HOT, H O T !*"

"*Very* lovely," admired Gabriel. "Now *I'll* get the pepper."

"I've been listening," mumbled Trumpet, coming out from under a pew bench.

"Never mind," fussed Peter, putting pepper in Gabriel's bottle of milk.

"*And* my stomach feels fine," went on Trumpet. "Perfectly *fine*."

"Don't interrupt," cried Peter, putting down the pepper pot. "Gabriel, have a lick of your milk!"

"It's so hot," said Gabriel tasting a bit, "that I can't have a lick!"

"That's hot enough," said Peter. "Lie down, Trumpet."

"Don't want to," pleaded Trumpet as Peter and Gabriel pushed him into a corner and put the milk bottle on the middle of his stomach.

"Oh, wow!" cried Trumpet. "You didn't put the stopper back! It's spilling all over me!

"Oh, I'll be burned!" cried Trumpet. "I'll be burned all over! Wow — wowl!!!"

"He's howling even louder," sighed Gabriel.

"And here comes Parson Pease-Porridge," fussed Peter.

"Parson Pease-Porridge is *running!*" cried Gabriel. "This time he'll be *sure* to send us away! Let's hide, Peter!"

"Oh, rack and ruin," exclaimed Parson Pease-Porridge, when he saw Trumpet. "Heavenly days! *Now* you're all covered with milk! You'll be the botheration of me! Tut, tut, tut, I shall *have* to give you another bath!"

"Lack-a-day, but I never knew such a small dog could need so much pink soap," sighed Parson Pease-Porridge, scrubbing away on poor Trumpet.

"Peter," whispered Gabriel, "you make a poem about it."

"I shall," said Peter, lifting his eyebrows ——

> "Oh,
> Pink soap tastes
> Just fine to me,
> But Trumpet hates it.
> Tra-la la-lee!"

"Inspiring!" breathed Gabriel. "I could just listen and listen!"

Next day Trumpet stayed behind the organ but Peter and Gabriel could hear him howling just the same.

"*I* know what," cried Gabriel. "Trumpet has a headache!"

"True, true," agreed Peter. "A frightful headache!"

"Exactly," cried Gabriel. "And Parson Pease-Porridge *always* puts an ice-bag on a headache."

"So what?" said Peter. "We *haven't* any ice-bag."

"But, we *do* have that good hand-bag someone left under a pew bench," said Gabriel. "I'll get it."

"There isn't any ice in it," said Peter when Gabriel came back with the bag.

"There's other things in it though!" beamed Gabriel. "It'll do quite nicely."

"Haven't any headache," grumbled Trumpet, coming out from behind the organ. "Don't like bags either."

'You'll *like* this one," said Peter and Gabriel, popping the hand-bag on Trumpet's head before he could duck behind the organ again.

"Don't like it," shouted Trumpet. "Can't breathe! Something's in my nose! Help! Help!"

"It's only powder," explained Peter.

"Face powder," encouraged Gabriel, "It can't hurt a *bit*."

"Don't care," shouted Trumpet. "It smells like pink soap. It's in my eyes too, and I can't see at all! Oh, wow-ow-owl!"

Then Parson Pease-Porridge came a-running!

"Dear-o-dearie," cried Parson Pease-Porridge when he saw Trumpet. "*Now* you have a hand-bag on your head! And you're covered with powder. However can such a little dog get into such big trouble?"

"I suppose," sighed Parson Pease-Porridge, sadly shaking his head, "that I *must* give you *another* bath."

"Do you think Trumpet had a headache, after all?" wondered Gabriel.

"Probably not," said Peter, lifting his eyebrows ——

"But ——
It seems to me
That Parson P.
Will have a headache."

"How sad," admired Gabriel. "How *very* sad."

"Listen," frowned Gabriel. "Trumpet's doing it *again!*"

"Only louder," fussed Peter.

"Something terrible must be happening," whispered Gabriel.

"Maybe measles," decided Peter.

"Maybe what?" asked Trumpet, who was away under Parson Pease-Porridge's desk.

"I said, maybe measles," repeated Peter. "They're awful!"

"And he's got those three big spots!" cried Gabriel, staring at Trumpet's back. "Oh, how sad! Parson Pease-Porridge says that with measles you always stay in a *dark* room."

"A dark room," mused Peter. "We haven't any dark room —"

"And I'm afraid of the dark," interrupted Trumpet. "Besides, my spots feel fine!"

"But, we *have* a nice dark coal scuttle," continued Peter, "that has good dark coal in it."

"The very thing," cried Gabriel. "We'll get it."

"This won't hurt at all," encouraged Peter as Gabriel helped him turn the coal scuttle up-side-down.

"Not at all," agreed Gabriel as they pushed poor Trumpet so far under the scuttle that only his tail stuck out!

"It's dark in here," wailed Trumpet, banging about in the coal scuttle.

"True, true," agreed Peter and Gabriel from the top of the scuttle. "Dark's the *surest* cure for measles!"

"It's *too* dark in here," wailed Trumpet even louder. "I want to come out! Hower-owl!"

"Oh, very well," fussed Peter. "Parson Pease-Porridge will let you out — "

"While we hide under a pew bench," whispered Gabriel. "Come on, Peter."

"I'll be twitched," cried Parson Pease-Porridge who came a-running. "Whatever has got under my coal scuttle?"

"Upon my soul," sputtered Parson Pease-Porridge. "It's Trumpet! Black with coal dust!"

"So," sighed Parson Pease-Porridge, "I must get the pink soap again."

"The pink soap!" whispered Peter. "Parson Pease-Porridge will use it all up before I ever get a bit."

"Too true," whispered Gabriel.

"You know what?" said Peter to Gabriel.

"No," said Gabriel.

"You haven't *noticed* anything?" asked Peter.

"No," said Gabriel, "I haven't."

"Well, I have," said Peter, lifting his eyebrows. "Trumpet *isn't* howling at all today."

"So he isn't," gasped Gabriel.

"Now, ask me why," urged Peter lifting his eyebrows even higher.

"All right," answered Gabriel, "Why? Why isn't he?"

"Because," cried Peter, "he has a sore throat, probably!"

"A sore throat!" gasped Gabriel. "Oh, poor Trumpet! We *must* put a wool sock around his neck."

"Exactly," said Peter, waving his arms. "One of Parson Pease-Porridge's wool socks!"

"Quite right," agreed Gabriel. "I know where to find a big one!"

"But my neck feels fine," came Trumpet's voice from under the last pew bench. "It feels perfect!"

"Never mind that," panted Gabriel as he came back, dragging Parson Pease-Porridge's best Sunday sock.

"We'll tie it tight," worried Peter. "Good and tight."

"What for?" grumbled Trumpet, backing away.

"So it can't come off, of course," said Gabriel.

"No," cried Trumpet, backing even farther under the pew bench. "I won't have it! My neck feels fine! *Fine*!!"

"Hold still," fussed Peter, helping Gabriel tie the sock around Trumpet's neck.

"And *please* stop shouting," cried Gabriel, "because I hear Parson Pease-Porridge coming."

"Don't care," wheezed Trumpet trying to pull the sock off his neck. "Don't like it! It's *too* tight! Now my neck does hurt! Somebody take it off! Help, help! Oh, owl wowl!!"

"I'll be twitched," panted Parson Pease-Porridge when he came a-running. "Everything happens to me at once! I must find out what all this noise is about even if I can't find my other best wool sock!"

"For pity's sakes," whispered Peter, peering over the hymn book he had hidden behind, "Parson Pease-Porridge has on only *one* sock!"

"Quite right," whispered Gabriel, peering over another hymn book. "It's the mate to the one I took!"

"How awful!" gasped Peter. *"Now* Parson Pease-Porridge will be *sure* to send us away!"

"I'll be twitched," panted Parson Pease-Porridge, looking behind the organ and under the pulpit. "Where *is* that noise coming from? I'll find out if I have to look under *every* last pew bench!"

"Upon my soul!" gasped Parson Pease-Porridge when he looked under the very last pew bench. "Trumpet! *Trumpet!!* And you're wearing my other best wool sock! Oh, but I'm the bothered old body!"

"Give it to me, I say," cried Parson Pease-Porridge pulling hard on the sock. "Dear, o-dearie you seem to be eating it, too. You have the whole toe ——!"

"Well, bless my soul," exclaimed Parson Pease-Porridge, trying to take the toe from Trumpet. "It seems to be caught on something — !"

"Why, it's caught on a tooth," cried Parson Pease-Porridge, pushing up his spectacles and peering into Trumpet's mouth.

"A brand-new tooth!" smiled Parson Pease-Porridge. "No wonder you've been a bother. And no wonder you've been howling! You've been cutting a tooth!!"

"Tut, tut, tut," went on Parson Pease-Porridge. "Just think of it! A tooth! We *must* celebrate, but let me see now — *first* you shall have a nice bath!!"

"But *not* with pink soap," smiled Peter, as Parson Pease-Porridge hurried away with Trumpet.

"Why not?" asked Gabriel.

"*Because,*" smiled Peter.

"Why didn't you tell us you had a brand-new tooth?" fussed Peter.

"You didn't ask me," answered Trumpet. "Besides, I only had it today."

"It's a lovely big tooth," admired Gabriel. "Make a poem about it, Peter."

"No," fussed Peter, "I'm not in the mood."

"Then *I* shall," smiled Trumpet. "Would anyone care to hear it ——"

"No," shouted Peter, "*I* always make up the poems."

"*Please,*" begged Trumpet. "Just this once."

"Oh, very well," said Peter. "Just this once."

"We're listening," beamed Gabriel.

"Thank you," said Trumpet, lifting his eyebrows the way Peter always did when *he* made up a poem ——

"My brand-new tooth
    Looks nice on me,
      On me, on me,
      On me, on me,
        On ——

"Oh-h," gasped Trumpet. "Excuse me please, I just remembered something *important*. Parson Pease-Porridge gave me a big bone to chew with my new tooth, but he didn't give me a bath after all ———"

"I know," said Peter. "Parson Pease-Porridge couldn't find the pink soap."

"Why not?" asked Gabriel.

"Because," whispered Peter, "I *ate* it!"

THE END

THE THREE
SILLY KITTENS

THE THREE SILLY KITTENS

Once there were three silly kittens named Tom, Dick, and Harry.

One day said Tom to Dick, "Where's Harry?"

"I'm right here," said Harry, "behind this big book."

"What are you doing behind a big book?" said Tom and Dick. "*You* can't read."

"I know it," answered Harry.

"You can't even spell," said Tom.

"I know it," said Harry.

"You can't even tell what page it is," cried Dick.

"I know it, I know it." answered Harry.

"Then," cried Tom and Dick, "you're silly."

"I am not," shouted Harry. "I don't have to read. I don't have to spell. I don't have to know what page it is."

"Why not?" cried Tom and Dick.

"Because," beamed Harry, "it's a picture book and I'm only *looking!* Now who's silly?"

WHAT ARE STAIRS FOR?

"What are stairs for?" asked Harry one day.

"That *is* a good question," said Tom, "but I wouldn't know the answer."

"I wouldn't either," said Dick.

"Well, my stars," said Harry, "don't give up. Let's play run-up-the-stairs while we think about it."

"Good!" said Dick.

"Very good," said Tom.

So up the stairs they all went as fast as they could.

"Now," said Harry, "do you know what stairs are for?"

"Not yet," said Dick and Tom. "That's a very hard question. Let's play run-down-the-stairs while we think some more."

So *down* the stairs they all went as fast as they could.

"*Now,* do you know what stairs are for?" said Harry to Tom and Dick.

"Of course we do," said Tom. "It just came to us!"

"Stairs are to run down after you run up," said Dick. "That's what stairs are for!"

"Quite right," said Harry. "How *very* smart you are!"

"Do you now what I look like?"

"Of course," answered Tom and
like a kitten."

"No, I don't" said Dick. "I

"*You do not,*" said Tom

"I do, too," said Dick,
Just like a horse."

"Oh, well then," sa
a *cow*."

"Why do you look

"Because," said H
a cow."

"If that's true,"
chair."

"Like a chair!"

"That's right,

"Don't be so
like a chair."

"So you don'

"Yes, I do,'
a chair has fo

TOM'S GARDEN

4

"I'm tired of falling down," said Dick.

"I am, too," said Harry. "It's getting so you can't walk anywhere without falling into a hole!"

"Tom!" cried Dick. "Whatever are you doing digging up the lawn?"

"I'm making a garden," answered Tom. "I'll have lots of flowers and lots of vegetables."

"You will not," cried Dick and Harry. "You're only burying a lot of old magazines in holes. Old magazines won't grow!"

"These aren't old magazines," said Tom. "These are catalogues."

"Catalogues!" cried Dick and Harry. "Aren't you foolish? Anyone knows you have to plant seeds to make things grow."

"I know it," said Tom. "That's why I'm planting *seed* catalogues. *Now,* who's foolish?"

"Dick," said Harry, "please step over here!"

"What for?" asked Dick.

"I just want you to see what Tom is doing now," said Harry.

"For heaven's sake!" cried Dick. "*Tom!* What *are* you doing?"

"Anyone can see what I'm doing," answered Tom, breaking an egg into a bucket of paint. "I'm coloring eggs for Easter."

"That's not the way to do it," cried Dick. "Nobody colors the insides of eggs!"

"They don't?" cried Tom in great surprise.

"Of course not," said Harry, "Only the *outsides,* you silly."

"Well, then," smiled Tom, reaching for another egg, "I guess that's easy to do, too."

"Indeed!" said Dick and Harry.

"Like this," said Tom, breaking the egg and dropping the *shells* into the paint. "I'll just color the *outsides,* instead. So you see I'm not such a silly. We'll have a nice Easter after all."

5

DICK'S CLOCK

"My, my, what a fine big clock," said Tom.

"Thank you," said Dick. "I found it right here on the table."

"Indeed!" said Harry.

"Now, why don't you ask me what time it is?" smiled Dick.

"All right," said Harry. "What time is it, please?"

"It's twelve o'clock noon," answered Dick.

"How do you know?" cried Tom.

"*You* can't tell time," cried Harry.

"Of course I can't," beamed Dick.

"Why, you're not even looking at the clock," cried Harry.

"Of course I'm not," said Dick.

"You're just standing on it," cried Tom.

"It doesn't make a bit of difference," smiled Dick.

"Then how do you know it's twelve o'clock noon?" shouted Tom and Harry.

"It's very easy," said Dick. "I had my breakfast hours ago and now I'm hungry again. So it *must* be twelve o'clock noon."

"*Lunch time!*" cried Tom and Harry.

THE KITTENS CLIMB A TREE

"I'd like to do something daring today," said Tom. "I feel very brave."

"The air *is* bracing," said Dick, thumping his chest. "I feel brave too."

"So do I," said Harry thumping *his* chest and turning a somersault. "I feel so brave that I could do most anything! I'm going to climb a *big tree!*"

"That's the spirit," cried Tom. "Only, I don't think I feel *that* brave."

"Neither do I," said Dick.

"Well then," said Harry, "I'll climb a little tree."

"That's better," said Tom. "Here's a little tree just our size."

"Much better," cried Dick. "Let's *all* start climbing"

"Fine," said Harry, and up the little tree they scrambled.

"I climbed to the top!" shouted Tom.

"I climbed to the middle!" shouted Dick.

"And *I* climbed to the bottom!" shouted poor Harry.

FISHING

"Hello," called Tom and Dick, who were lying in the shade of an old apple tree. "Where are you going with that bucket and fish pole?"

"Hello, hello!" answered Harry. "I'm going fishing. You could come along if you weren't so lazy."

"What for?" yawned Dick. "You can't catch a fish in a bucket!"

"I know it," answered Harry.

"*You* couldn't catch a fish in a bucket even if it had water in it," added Tom.

"I know it," answered Harry.

"Then why should we come along?" said Tom and Dick, rolling over on their backs.

"Because," smiled Harry, "I'm not going to fish in my bucket. My bucket is full of lunch!"

"Lunch!" shouted Tom and Dick, jumping to their feet.

"That's right," beamed Harry. "*Now* would you like to come along, you stupids!"

"We certainly would," cried Tom and Dick. "Wait up for us!"

MUD PIES

"My, what beautiful pies!" said Tom.

"I'm glad you think so," said Harry.

"Gorgeous," said Dick. "My mouth simply waters."

"Fine," said Harry, "because I made them just for you and Tom."

"Oh, thank you!" cried Tom, grabbing a pie and taking a big bite.

"Oh, thank you *so* much," cried Dick, grabbing the other pie and biting a big piece out of it.

"Oh-h-h!" cried Tom dropping his pie.

"Oh, ugh-h-h!" cried Dick dropping his pie, too. "They don't taste good at all!"

"Of course they don't," said Harry.

"Why don't they?" cried Tom.

"Pies *should* taste good," shouted Dick.

"Not these pies," said Harry. "You're not supposed to eat them!"

"Not supposed to eat them!" shouted Tom.

"Why not?" shouted Dick.

"Because," smiled Harry, "they're *mud* pies. They're only to look at!"

TOM PAINTS A PICTURE

"Come over here, Dick," said Harry. "Tom's making a picture."

"A picture!" cried Dick, hurrying over. "Oh, I *like* pictures!"

"Most everyone does," said Tom.

"And that's a fine big one you're painting," said Dick, peering over Tom's shoulder.

"Isn't it, though?" said Tom with a modest smile.

"What's it going to be?" inquired Harry.

"Oh, I don't know," said Tom, daubing away with his yellow and red and blue paint.

"You don't know!" cried Dick and Harry.

"No, I don't," answered Tom, daubing on a bit more paint.

"Well then, you're foolish." cried Dick. "Because if you don't know what you're painting, you won't know when you're finished!"

"Yes, I will, too, know when I'm finished," answered Tom."

"*How* will you know?" asked Dick and Harry.

"That's easy," smiled Tom, "I'll be finished when my paint jars are all *empty!*"

TOM'S UMBRELLA

"Look at Tom!" shouted Dick.

"For goodness' sake," sighed Harry. "He's being silly again."

"Tom!" hollered Dick, "where did you get that old worn-out umbrella?"

"I found it," answered Tom.

"It's no good," said Harry. "It's full of holes."

"I know," said Tom.

"Well, you *are* stupid," said Dick. "It's beginning to rain and you'll get wet!"

"No, I won't," smiled Tom.

"You won't?" cried Dick and Harry. "Then we want to get under your umbrella, too."

"Fine," said Tom, "only you'll have to hold it."

"Why should we hold your old umbrella?" cried Dick and Harry.

"Because," said Tom, handing them his umbrella, "*I* only stand under my umbrella when the sun shines. When it rains I run under the porch. That's why I don't get wet. *Now* who's stupid?"

"Well," said Dick and Harry, clutching the old umbrella, "I guess we are."

SLEDDING

"That's a nice sled you have there," said Dick, tagging Harry up the hill.

"Indeed it is," answered Harry. "It's fast as a comet."

"I'll bet it's *so* fast," said Tom, tagging along behind Dick, "that we'll all be down the hill before we even know we started."

"No, we won't," said Harry.

"Of course we will," said Tom.

"No *we* won't," said Harry.

"Why not?" asked Dick and Tom.

"Because," cried Harry, when they reached the top of the hill, "my sled is only big enough for me. Everybody get out of my way. . . . Here I go! Whe-e-e!"

"Ha! Ha!" shouted Dick, jumping right on Harry's back. "And here I go, too. Whe-e-e-e!"

"Ho! ho!" hollered Tom, jumping right on Dick's back, "And here goes me!"

"Whe-e-e-e! Whe-e-e! Whe-e-e!"

THE TEA PARTY

"Tom, will you stop tramping around," cried Dick. "I'm trying to have a nap."

"Oh, very sorry," said Tom.

"*And,*" shouted Harry, "*please* stop rattling those dishes. Whatever are you doing?"

"Can't you see?" smiled Tom. "I'm having a tea party."

"A tea party," cried Dick. "My stars! Kittens don't have tea parties."

"Certainly not," said Harry. "We don't even *like* tea."

"Well, *I* do," said Tom. "Tea is fine. With cream and sugar."

"*Cream!*" cried Dick, scrambling to his feet.

"*Sugar!*" cried Harry, scrambling up, too. "That's different!"

"Isn't it though?" said Tom. "Do sit down again."

"Indeed we will," said Dick and Harry, reaching for cups and saucers.

"And *now,*" said Tom, "I'll pour you some tea."

"No, you won't," cried Dick and Harry, filling their cups with sugar and cream, "we'll just have our tea *without any tea at all.* And thank you."

THE END

GABRIEL CHURCHKITTEN
AND THE MOTHS

GABRIEL AND THE MOTHS

"Listen!" said Gabriel Churchkitten.

"I am," said Peter Churchmouse.

"You are not," said Trumpet Churchdog. "You're playing run-up-the-candlestick."

"Oh, fuss!" said little Peter, scrambling down the candlestick. "For pity's sake, what is it?"

"Oh, it's *so* terrible!" cried Gabriel. "Parson Pease-Porridge is going to get a *new cat!*"

"A new cat!" gulped Peter. "What for?"

"Because I'm *moth-eaten,*" whispered Gabriel.

"Moth-eaten!" cried Peter, staring at Gabriel. "I don't believe it!"

"Well, that's the way we heard it," shouted Trumpet. "Parson Pease-Porridge said, *'I'm going to get a new cat because my old cat's moth-eaten!'*"

"Isn't that sad for me?" sighed Gabriel. "Now, I suppose Parson Pease-Porridge will have to give *me* away!"

"Did you say give *you* away?" cried Peter. "A fine big kitten like you?"

"Yes, I did," sighed Gabriel. "Isn't it a shame?"

"Indeed it is," said Peter. "My, your good fur coat must be *very* moth-eaten!"

"It must be," worried poor Gabriel. "And it's the only coat I have!"

"True, true," said Peter, lifting his eyebrows the way he always did when he made a little poem——

> "Oh, it's so sad
> And it's too bad
> Gabriel has
> Moths, moths, moths!"

"That's such a lovely poem that I wish I had moths, too," admired Trumpet. "I could just listen and listen and——

"It is *not* a lovely poem!" shouted Gabriel. "Nobody wants moths. They're awful!"

"Indeed," said Peter.

"I have an *idea*," said Peter after a while.

"What kind of an idea?" asked Gabriel, who was playing hide-in-the-wastebasket.

"The kind to keep moths out of your fur coat," said Peter as he climbed up on Parson Pease-Porridge's desk.

"Oh fine!" said Gabriel, scrambling out of the wastebasket. "Then Parson Pease-Porridge won't give me away."

"Good!" said Trumpet, scrambling out of the wastebasket, too. "Go on, Peter."

"Very well, then," said Peter. "Now, how does Parson Pease-Porridge keep moths out of things?"

"With moth balls, of course," answered Gabriel.

"Exactly," said Peter. "There's heaps of moth balls in the cupboard. Parson Pease-Porridge *even* puts them in his pockets!"

"Indeed he does," cried poor Gabriel. "But I can't keep moths out of me because *I* haven't any pockets and I *can't* hang my coat in the cupboard where the moth balls are either, because I'm in it!"

"How true," sighed Trumpet.

"Oh, do stop it!" cried Peter. "You don't need pockets and you don't need to hang your coat in the cupboard!"

"I don't?" cried Gabriel.

"Certainly not," said Peter, sliding Parson Pease-Porridge's glue pot to the edge of the desk, "All you need is a touch of this good glue."

"Glue?" cried Gabriel, staring up at Peter. "I hate glue. It'll make things stick on me!"

"Quite right," said Peter, tipping the pot and pouring glue all over Gabriel.

"Oh, now you've done it," cried Gabriel, staggering back. "Poor me! Oh, poor, poor me!"

"It's for your own good," said Peter. "So please stop fussing and get into the cupboard and roll in Parson Pease-Porridge's moth balls."

"I won't!" shouted Gabriel, stamping up and down in the glue.

"Yes-you-will-too!" said Trumpet, and he pushed Gabriel into the moth balls and slammed the cupboard door shut.

"Now roll, Gabriel, roll," encouraged Peter, "while I make a little poem about it ——

> Roll, roll, roll,
> Quick, quick, quick,
> Stick, stick, stick,
> Roll, stick, quick!"

"My, what a beautiful poem," admired Trumpet.

"Isn't it?" said Peter, "I'd make another only Gabriel is making such a fuss in the moth balls that Parson Pease-Porridge is sure to come a-running!"

"Heavenly days!" exclaimed Parson Pease-Porridge, when he came a-running. "Whatever is banging about in my cupboard?"

"I'll be twitched," cried Parson Pease-Porridge, pulling open the cupboard door, "it's Gabriel! Oh, ruination! What a sinful waste of glue and my good moth balls! One look at you, Gabriel, would frighten away every moth in the parish!"

Then Parson Pease-Porridge began to pluck moth balls off Gabriel and put them back in the cupboard.

"I believe some of your coat came off with the moth balls," said Peter.

"Indeed it did," said poor Gabriel. "In lots of places."

"And now you look worse than ever," said Trumpet.

"Precisely," said Peter. "Worse than ever."

"Oh, how sad for me!" cried Gabriel, staring at his ragged fur coat in the mirror over the organ, "*Now* what shall I do?"

"Listen to me, that's what," said Peter, lifting his eyebrows.

"Oh I know
What to do-de-do
To make your coat
As good as new——"

"You do?" broke in Gabriel.

"Don't interrupt," said Peter, waving his arms——

> "A daub here
> A daub there
> Where you're worn
> Or where you're bare
> Daub, daub, daub, daub!"

"What a beautiful thought," said Trumpet.

"Is it?" asked Gabriel.

"It is," answered Peter, "For Parson Pease-Porridge always daubs old worn-out candlesticks with the gold paint he keeps in the cupboard."

"Yes, he does," smiled Gabriel, "and they look like new."

"So," said Peter, "We'll daub you."

"That's it," shouted Trumpet, getting the gold paint and banging it so hard that the lid flew off. "Daub up Gabriel!"

"Daub up *me* with gold paint?" cried Gabriel backing under a hymn book, "*No!* I'd rather have moths!"

"Oh, don't be silly," said Peter, reaching into the gold.

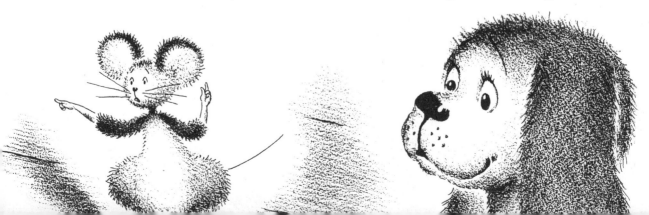

"You're simply lovely," said Trumpet when they finished daubing gold on Gabriel. "You shine like a candlestick."

"Very true," agreed Peter. "Do have a look in the mirror over the organ."

"I'm afraid to," said poor Gabriel.

"Oh, fiddlesticks!" said Peter. "Don't be so stubborn."

"One little look won't hurt you," said Trumpet, pushing Gabriel along.

"Oh, very well, then," said Gabriel, staring into the mirror.

"You see!" said Peter.

"Oh, my!" blinked Gabriel. "I *am* a gorgeous kitten now even if I am a bit moth-eaten! Parson Pease-Porridge will hardly know me!"

"How right you are," said Peter, as he followed Trumpet under a pew bench. Just as Parson Pease-Porridge came around the corner!

"I'll be twitched," said Parson Pease-Porridge, when he saw Gabriel shining like a candlestick. "You've been in my gold!"

"Oh my gold, my good gold!" groaned Parson Pease-Porridge. "Oh, but you'll be the ruination of me!"

"Parson Pease-Porridge knew me all right and he didn't like me daubed up like a candlestick at all," sniffed Gabriel holding his nose. "Parson Pease-Porridge used a whole bottle of his good Lilac hair tonic to take the gold off me, and now besides being moth-eaten I smell terrible!"

"I wonder how long it takes Lilac to go away?" asked Trumpet, holding his nose, too.

"That, I cannot say," replied Peter, keeping as far away from Gabriel as he could. "However if you will open a window, perhaps I can think of another plan —"

"To keep Parson Pease-Porridge from giving me away even though I am moth-eaten?" sighed Gabriel as he helped Trumpet open a window.

"That's it," said Peter.

"Oh, I do like plans," said Trumpet. "Let's hear your plan, Peter."

"Very well," said Peter, taking a deep breath. "Now, Parson Pease-Porridge is very dignified, isn't he? Even if he had moths you wouldn't notice it."

"That's true," said Gabriel. "And Parson Pease-Porridge says dignity is *very* important."

"Correct," said Peter. "So if you were dignified like *me*, for instance, Parson-Pease-Porridge wouldn't *think* of giving you away, would he?"

"I suppose not," sighed poor Gabriel.

"Well, you could be dignified if your tail weren't so short," said Peter staring at Gabriel. "My tail is long."

"And very dignified," finished Trumpet.

"But we can't make *my* tail any longer," cried Gabriel.

"Oh, yes we can," said Peter.

"How?" asked Gabriel in despair.

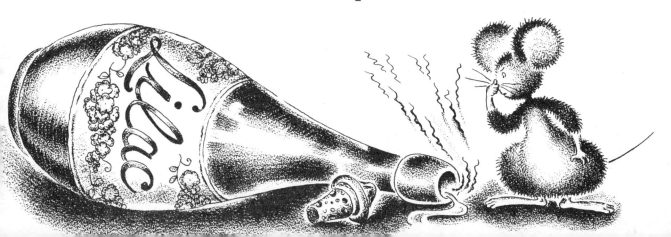

"With one of Parson Pease-Porridge's foot-warmers of course," said Peter. "Follow me!"

"A foot-warmer!" cried Gabriel as he followed Peter under Parson Pease-Porridge's bed. "Oh, poor me!"

"Courage, Gabriel, courage," shouted Trumpet, dragging one of the foot-warmers under the bed after him.

"Now what?" asked Gabriel, eyeing the foot-warmer. "It's too flat and draggy."

"It won't be when we stuff it with something," said Peter, biting a hole in the bottom of Parson Pease-Porridge's mattress. "We won't need much," went on Peter, pulling out a big piece of stuffing and pushing it into the toe of the foot-warmer.

"And Parson Pease-Porridge will hardly miss it," said Trumpet as he helped Peter.

"It does begin to shape up," admired Gabriel when the foot-warmer was round instead of flat.

"Quite right," said Peter. "And *now* we'll try it for size."

"It fits like a glove," said Trumpet pulling the foot-warmer over Gabriel's tail.

"It stays on like a glove, too," said Peter, fastening the strings. "And it's very becoming."

"Oh, I must be handsome!" said Gabriel, sitting up straight and looking *very* dignified. "Now Parson Pease-Porridge could never think of giving me away!"

"Oh, where, oh, where has my foot-warmer gone?"
hummed Parson Pease-Porridge when he was ready for
bed, "Oh, where, oh, where, can it be? Oh, but I'm the
bothered old body and I just can't get my sleep at all until
I find my other foot-warmer!"

"Now is the time!" whispered Peter, giving Gabriel's
new tail a final jerk. "Step right out!"

"And let Parson Pease-Porridge see how dignified you
look," said Trumpet, pushing Gabriel from under the
bed.

"Heavenly days!" cried Parson Pease-Porridge when
he saw Gabriel and the foot-warmer. "Playing tricks
again!"

"Oh, what a way you are!" cried Parson Pease-
Porridge, staring at Gabriel's new tail, "However did
you get into my good foot-warmer?

"Dear-oh-dearie, I'm afraid I'll never understand
you," cried Parson Pease-Porridge, catching Gabriel and
untying his new tail.

"Dearie-oh-dearie-me," sighed Parson Pease-Porridge,
shaking the stuffing out of the foot-warmer. "Dearie, but
such goings on do make me weary."

Then Parson Pease-Porridge put on his foot-warmer
and got right into bed and was soon fast asleep.

"Parson Pease-Porridge thought I was playing tricks and he didn't notice that I was dignified at all," cried Gabriel.

"Quite right," agreed Peter.

"How sad it all is!" sighed Gabriel. "Parson Pease-Porridge will give me away for *sure!*"

"We're going to miss you, Gabriel," said Trumpet, wiping away a tear.

"Indeed we are," said Peter, looking sadly at Gabriel.

"Oh, poor me," sobbed Gabriel as he curled up in the collection basket. "Oh poor moth-eaten me."

Next morning there was a big striped box on Parson Pease-Porridge's desk.

"I like new boxes," said Trumpet, jumping up on the box. "What do you suppose is in it?"

"I don't know," said Gabriel, jumping up beside Trumpet.

"Well, I do," cried Peter, waving his arms. "I'll even try to make a little poem about it ——

> C-C-C-ccc
> C-C-C-aaa
> C-C-C-A-A-ttt
> C A T !"

"*Cat!*" cried Gabriel and Trumpet together.

"Of course," gasped Peter. "*The new cat!*"

163

"Oh, poor me," cried Gabriel. "Oh, poor, poor, me. Oh-poor-me!"

"Don't just stand there saying 'Oh-poor-me!'" said Peter. "*Do* something!"

"Gladly," said Gabriel, giving the box a terrible bang. "Hello in there! What's your name?"

"That's right, Gabriel," shouted Peter. "What does he say?"

"He doesn't seem to answer," replied Gabriel.

"He must be deaf," said Trumpet. "Why don't we look inside?"

"Very well," said Peter, jumping up on the box and biting the ribbon in two. "Now, you can shove the lid off."

"My!" said Trumpet. "Isn't Peter brave?"

"Indeed he is," agreed Gabriel, shoving the lid. "The new cat has probably *never* seen a churchmouse!"

"What a dreadful thought!" cried little Peter, jumping behind a candlestick just as the lid fell off.

"Come back, Peter," said Gabriel, peering into the box. "There isn't any cat. It's only a hat!"

"That's different," said Peter, climbing back up on the box. "I don't mind hats at all."

"Fine," said Gabriel. "Then perhaps you won't mind biting a hole in it?"

"Not at all," said Peter, "But what for?"

"So we can see inside," said Gabriel. "Because the new cat *must* be under the hat."

"For pity's sake," cried Peter, scrambling off the box again and up the candlestick. "Oh fuss, fuss, fuss!"

"Come back here, Peter," cried Gabriel. "We'll *sit* on the hat while you bite a hole in it. You'll be quite safe."

"True, true," said Peter, coming back and bravely biting into the big hat.

"How splendid," admired Trumpet as the felt began to fly. "Only it isn't *quite* big enough!"

"Not quite," said Gabriel, trying to see in the hole.

"Oh, but it will be," said Peter, biting away till the hole was almost as big as he was, "*Now* can you see?"

"No," said Gabriel. "Bite it bigger, please."

"I'll be glad to," said Peter. And he bit the hole so big that he fell right into it!

"Oh save me quick!" shouted Peter. "Help, help, help!!"

"Please be calm," cried Gabriel. "We'll save you as soon as we can get into the hole you bit."

"It's hard to do because we're so big," explained Trumpet.

"Oh, never mind," came Peter's voice from inside the hat. "Kindly get off the hole so that I can climb out!"

"Gladly," said Gabriel and Trumpet together.

"There's no one in there at all!" said Peter, coming out of the hole. "There was only me!"

"Can you imagine that?" said Trumpet, tugging the hat out of the box and looking inside it. "No one at all!"

"Well, there will be soon," said Gabriel, climbing into the hat. "It's just big enough for a nice bed. I like it much better than the collection basket and besides I won't have to get up so early on Sunday morning!"

"Then, it's too bad that I had to bite the big hole in it," said Peter. "Because your tail sticks out."

"Oh, I don't mind that," smiled Gabriel, settling down and closing his eyes. "I like it here. It's so-o-o cozy."

"Maybe Parson Pease-Porridge will even think Gabriel is the new cat!" whispered Trumpet.

"Perhaps," whispered Peter, looking at Gabriel who was already fast asleep. "But we'd better get under a hymn book because Parson Pease-Porridge is coming!"

169

"Heavenly days!" exclaimed Parson Pease-Porridge when he saw Gabriel fast asleep in the hat.

"It's Gabriel again!" cried Parson Pease-Porridge who didn't for a moment think Gabriel was a new cat.

"Oh, but I'm a ruined old man!" cried Parson Pease-Porridge, wringing his hands. "Oh, my new hat! Gabriel has made a bed of it! He even has a hole for his tail to stick out!"

"Dear-oh-dear," sighed Parson Pease-Porridge, sadly shaking his head. "It seems that I'm not to have a new hat after all."

"Hem-mmp! I must make the best of it," said Parson Pease-Porridge as he took his old moth-eaten hat from the cupboard and placed it firmly on his head.

"Ah me," smiled Parson Pease-Porridge as he softly closed the door behind him. "Perhaps old friends are the best friends after all — *even* when they're a bit moth-eaten!"

"Wake up, Gabriel!" shouted Peter.

"What for?" yawned Gabriel.

"Because," scowled Peter, "you didn't hear Parson Pease-Porridge say he was going to get a new cat at all."

"I didn't?" said Gabriel rubbing his eyes.

"*You did not,*" replied Peter. "Parson Pease-Porridge said he was going to get a new hat."

"Not a new cat?" broke in Gabriel.

"*No,*" said Peter. "*A new hat.* Because his old hat was all moth-eaten."

"Well," said Gabriel, "I guess Parson Pease-Porridge won't have to give me away after all."

"I suppose we just heard wrong," said Trumpet. "HAT does sound an awful lot like CAT!"

"*Anyone* could make a mistake like that," smiled Gabriel.

"Indeed!" said Peter.

THE END